Moonlight Sonata Op. 27 in C# BDSM

steamy paranormal romance, Volume 2

Saskia Lane

Published by Vital Books Inc, 2023.

MOONLIGHT SONATA OP. 27 IN C# BDSM

First edition. October 31, 2023.

Copyright © 2023 Saskia Lane.

ISBN: 979-8223267812

Written by Saskia Lane.

Also by Saskia Lane

cruising for alphas
Taxi Driver Hot Wife
Taxi Driver Hot Wife 2

steamy paranormal romance
Riding a Monster Wave at BDSM Beach
Moonlight Sonata Op. 27 in C# BDSM

Steamy Trials of a Victorian Lady
In His Lordship's Dovecote
In His Lordship's House of Ill Fame
In Their Lordships' Dungeon

Standalone
Where's My Bikini Bottom? And Other Stories
Where's My Bikini Bottom? And Other Stories
Thanks For The Hotpants, Lieutenant
Explicit Creatures on a Hot Night

The Explicit End of the Beach
Losing my V-card with the Wrong Alpha
Getting a Job in My Mom's Boyfriend's Sex Club
Ouch! That Sand's Hot and This Alpha Stud's Too Big

CHAPTER ONE: GETTING READY FOR THE LESSON

... dah dah dah dah dah dah dah dah dah dah dah dah

Nine o'clock in the morning! What a freaking time to be playing the *Moonlight* Sonata!

... dah dah dah dah dah dah dah dah dah dah dah dah

Stuck here sitting at my family's Steinway piano, morning sunlight streaming through the gold-embroidered swags of our bespoke curtains practicing Beethoven's *homage to moonlight!*

... Moonlight lapping on still water...

... Dah dah dah dah dah dah dah dah dah dah dah dah...

... The full moon shining down on a tranquil lake...

That's what my new piano teacher's set me for my first lesson! The Moonlight Sonata Op. 27 in C #! The simplest sonata in the classical repertoire! A piece I could play when I was three years old! I haven't even met my new teacher yet and I hate him already!

... dah dah dah dah dah dah dah dah dah dah dah dah...

Just because he's the world famous Herr Maxim Steinhammer, the foremost virtuoso of our day, doesn't mean I have to play this childishly easy stuff again and again and again, does it? I'M A VIRTUOSO TOO! I've performed in front of big audiences too! I've played in Carnegie Hall and l'Opera in Paris. I'm the youngest eighteen-year-old ever to win the Prix d'Or! I have an upcoming concert with the Philharmonia Orchestra in a fortnight. One day I'll be be a million times more famous than Herr Maxim Steinhammer!

... dah dah dah dah dah dah dah dah dah dah dah dah...

I've a good mind to tell Mama to phone and cancel him!

"Don't frown so, pet!" Mama's standing over me as usual making sure the maestro's instructions are carried out to the letter. It was Mama who booked my lesson with the nasty ogre. "You don't look nice when you scowl so fiercely!"

I'll scowl as much as I want! I'm stunning whether I'm scowling or not scowling! I'm 'nice' no matter how much hot resentment is coursing through my body. I'm not only talented, I'm beautiful too! Which is more than you can say for Herr Maxim. I've got film star good looks and a stunning body. Everybody says so. Fans swoon when I play Chopin, women fans as well as male fans. While Herr Steinhammer's a total fright. Have you seen seen his publicity pictures? The man's totally hideous.

I won't go! I'll make Mama cancel my lesson! I simply can't face the thought of sitting with such an ugly brute for an hour.

"Softer, darling. Play gently, Constantia. Herr Steinhammer says he wants you to play with feeling!"

"Go away, Mama! I can't stand it!"

"Just three more repetitions, pet. As slow as you can. Largo Maestoso. Herr Maxim says you're always in a rush. He says your Deutsche Gramaphon 'Songs Without Words' was 'a high speed train wreck.'"

DAH DAH DAH DAH DAH DAH DAH DAH DAH DAH DAH DAH

A high-speed train-wreck? I'll play as fast as I like. It's not up to him. *He* plays fast! Herr Steinhammer can take the most difficult music and play it at a hundred miles an hour without missing a single note! The Devil's blessed him— he's as ugly as the Devil— with extra long fingers and powerful hands just made for pounding out thunderous chords or making the back row audience of the biggest auditorium in the world hear a note on the edge of silence. That doesn't mean he can bully me! I could play the Moonlight Sonata when I was three freaking years old!

DAH DAH DAH DAH DAH DAH DAH DAH DAH DAH DAH DAH

"Please, Constantia. Calm down, cherie. You know what Herr Maxim's like!" My mother's the daughter of a Polish prince and even she's scared of Herr Maxim Steinhammer! "They say he can lose his temper so easily!"

Know what he's like? I've seen him! On record covers! On TV! At Madison Square Garden. Everybody's seen him! Ugly as sin. A complete fright of a man. Built like a steel rigger more than a musician. Dark smoldering eyes. That cruel, devouring mouth. The big hands. An ogre's bushy black beard.

I cry out: "Well he'd better not try and lose his temper with me!"

"Hush, pet. Quiet, Constantia. Don't say so. I'm sure your lesson will go very well. There's so much Herr Maxim can teach you! With the Philharmonia coming up! I'm sure you'll really enjoy your lesson once you get there. People say that Herr Steinhammer can be quite charming sometimes."

"Oh yes! I'm sure he can be charming when he wants to!"

The most hideous man imaginable and he's got women swooning all over him! Ladies young and old groveling at his feet! Supermodels. Celebrity actresses. Daughters of the nobility. Positively throwing themselves at him. Well not *this* daughter of the nobility, thank you very much.

People even say Herr Steinhammer has diabolical powers! Diabolical powers over women as much as over the keyboard. There are rumors that Herr Maxim has sold his soul to the Devil in return for his virtuoso technique and that when he plays the Moonlight Sonata he's possessed by the Devil Himself. People whisper that only the Devil can play with such fire and power. Audiences claim to have glimpsed flashes of hellfire spark from the keyboard when he plays the last movement, but that's just PR promotion stuff. It's all smoke and mirrors. The man's massively over-hyped.

DAH! DAH! DAH! DAH! DAH! DAH! DAH! DAH! DAH! DAH! DAH! DAH!

Moonlight lapping on freaking water at nine a.m on a sunny morning when you're dying to get out and go shopping, maybe a game of squash before lunch!

"Hurry up, Constantia! Your lesson's at eleven!"

"Hurry up, Mama? It isn't *hurry up* music!"

Luckily, a glimpse of my face in one of the many mirrors gracing our opulent drawing room reminds me of how beautiful I am, even more beautiful than usual this morning. An artfully tangled mane of silky blonde hair. Blue eyes of a lustrous brightness. Refined retroussé nose. Cherub lips of a juicy plumpness. The recent perfection of my voluptuous teenage body. With the way I play and my fabulous looks I'm going to be ten times more famous than Herr Maxim one day, and the hideous brute just can't stand it!

I smile back at myself in the mirror—playing this childish stuff you don't need to concentrate— and there it is, *my secret*, my own stunning mystery, more powerful than any Devil worship rubbish, there in *my face*, my *eyes*, my *lips*, my *hair*, in every pore of my stunning body, in my *heart* too, my heart as unravished as my voluptuous limbs, my soul as untried, by even a single man, as my breath-taking body. You see, I intend to remain a virgin. I'm going to stay unravished till I'm the greatest virtuoso ever, far greater than Herr Maxim Steinhammer, which makes it extra galling that I have to grind out this...

... *DAH! DAH! DAH! DAH! DAH! DAH! DAH! DAH! DAH!*...

SLAM!

"Constantia!"

I shut the piano. I slam the lid down. Two million dollars' worth of Steinway mahogany and steel strings jangles through the fluted columns and crystal chandeliers of our stately home.

"Constantia! Darling! Don't be like that. It's time for your lesson!"

CHAPTER TWO: FIRST MOVEMENT

ADAGIO SOSTENUTO. THE KEY TO THE OTHER WORLD

His rooms are dark. Memorial oak and smoke-stained teak. His apartment reeks of cigar smoke and whiskey. Candlelight quivers in brass sconces. Firelight trembles in the open hearth, even the flames seeming nervous of his ominous presence.

Candlelight?

Firelight?

An open hearth?

What a poser! The guy's an absolute fraud! Herr Maxim Steinhammer's worth millions. His concerts are sellouts. His CDs rake in a prince's ransom— and he pretends he's some impoverished romantic genius living in a garret, can't afford electricity!

The Steinway grand piano standing waiting for my lesson is worth nearly as much as my own.

He sits in a leather armchair, legs comfortably crossed, a big shoe kicking, carelessly cocked across his knee, the 'maestro' in his lair.

I realize how big he is, what a bulky body he has, brawny but ripped too. Even folded up in an armchair Herr Maxim's enormous. Six foot two if he's an inch. Broad, burly shoulders. Thighs as thick as tree trunks. *In a tuxedo!* Bow tie and tails! His muscular thighs encased in formal black with a silk stripe.

He looks me up and down.

A close-fitting, gray cashmere cocktail frock, bandeau neckline.

"So you're Constantia."

"That's me."

He's not *my* 'maestro.' My mother's a princess. My father's a member of parliament. I'm not about to let some self-important 'grandee of the keyboard' intimidate me.

He's sipping whiskey from faceted cut glass. He's a drinker.

Herr Maxim's famous for his drunken binges between concerts. He's notorious for getting into fights and trashing hotel rooms, but everyone makes excuses for him because he's a 'genius.' They say that he can even perform when intoxicated, thunder out a note-perfect 'Hammerklavier Sonata' to collapse in an inebriated heap as the applause rings out. It's all part of the hype. He's only a puffed-up PR phenomenon, he's not a genius at all.

He smiles at the scores I've brought to play for him, Brahms and Rachmaninov and Liszt, the difficult pieces I've brought to impress him with.

"So. Our up-and-coming young star!"

He says 'young' as if I'm nine years old. He dwells on 'up-and-coming' as if I'm some hopeless wannabe. He rolls 'star' around in his mouth with his whiskey, as if 'star' is the most ridiculous thing you can possibly call a beautiful young woman.

"If you say so, sir. I hope my playing does credit to the masterpieces I chose."

I nod at the scores I've brought along, Brahms. Tchaikovsky. Rachmaninov. I can handle difficult pieces as well as him.

He growls:

"I'm sure it does."

He glances sidelong at my face.

"I'm sure you look extremely hot on a record cover too, Constantia. Quite sexy on the cover of a music magazine."

I'm stunned!

"Messers Brahms, Tchaikovsky and Rachmaninov would no doubt have fallen head over heels in love with your playing if they'd had the good fortune to check out your hot little ass."

My mouth drops open.

I go hot all over.

It's appalling! Abominable! I've never been spoken to like this in my whole life! The ignorant pig!

It's all I can do not to stamp my foot and turn straight round and walk straight out again. I blurt:

"They can fall head over heels for me as much as they like, Herr Steinhammer, it's only their music I'll ever love!"

His eyes burn into me. He gives me a wry smile:

"Yes. Of course."

He knows I'm a virgin. His burning gaze finds out my poor secret, that my 'hot little ass' has never been tried, that my sexy body has never been ravished, that in fact I've never fucked a man. I do look hot on record covers, I do look fuck-able in music magazines, but I save all my desire for my music. He sees right through me. It shouldn't make me feel so vulnerable and nervous, but it does.

His ugly face creases in a hideous grin.

"You think the Moonlight Sonata is beneath you. Too childish. You could play it when you were three."

He sees into my mind as well as my heart! He knows exactly what I'm thinking!

I'm mumbling like a nervous school-girl:

"... I... I just... hoped I might play you something a little more challenging..."

"More challenging? There's nothing more challenging than the Moonlight Sonata!"

Suddenly I'm screaming. I can't breathe. A wild scream gets caught in my throat.

A fizz of black electricity jolts the room.

Darkness statics shivery lightning from armchair to piano.

One instant his huge body is coiled up in the armchair, the next it's seated at the piano, his tuxedo-d bulk transported through thin air like a springing panther's aura.

Before I can scream again, he begins to play.

... dah dah dah dah dah dah dah dah dah dah dah dah...

The water lapping my eyes is real, actual water, tranquil and fathomlessly deep.

... dah dah dah dah dah dah dah dah dah dah dah dah...

The moonlight shining on the water is real moonlight, extinguishing his terrified candle flames, snuffing out his shaking firelight.

... dah dah dah dah dah dah dah dah dah dah dah dah...

As he plays, his voice comes to me across a lake of brimming light.

"... The Moonlight Sonata, Constantia.. it isn't just notes on a page... even just the notes Beethoven wrote..." His guttural voice grows soft and gentle. His growl turns mystical. "... It's the shining path across the water... the Key to the Other Side..."

I want to make a scathing reply, snort out that I'm not deceived by hypnotic words, I'm not impressed by mystical claptrap, except I'm crying. My shoulders are shaking. Big sobs are rising up from deep inside me. A sorrow I never even knew I had within me is shuddering my body and trickling down my cheeks.

"... If you wish to be a great musician, Constantia, you must go to the Other Side..."

I wrap my arms around myself, hold on tight, but the water is rising above my head. The moonlight is blinding me. The sorrow is unbearable.

"The Other Side of what?"

His voice laps gently at my ears.

"Of everything, Constantia."

When he rises from the keyboard his face is beautiful. His ugliness is gone. He stands above me—it's impossible to tell whether he's finished playing or not— his features filled with splendor. His crude lips and gross nose and cruel eyes are just the same as they were a moment ago but now a radiant luster is shining forth from them.

He takes me in his arms, his eyes an angel's thrown out of heaven, his lips a seraph's denied the Waters of Life. My arms go round his neck. His broad, stunning lips batten on mine.

The luscious lightning of his angel's tongue fills my mouth, grapples with my tongue in succulent combat. He may be a fallen angel but I adore him. He can be Lucifer Himself, I no longer care. I taste paradise. The tang of paradise mingles with my voluptuous saliva. Thank God I saved my love. Thank heavens I waited for this breath-taking kiss.

"... Mm... mm-mmmmmmm... mm-mmmmmmmmmmmmmmm..."

I drown in his kiss. His arms are around me, pulling me under, radiant water flowing over my breasts, a moonlit tide streaming down my cleavage, his hands inside my bandeau neckline, the fingers that hammer out Brahms and Beethoven and Tchaikovsky plundering my sumptuous softness, the fingertips that stroke ecstasy from black keys and white keys gouging my shapely fullness, pinching my nipples so hard I cry out:

"... Ow...!"

'Ow!' gets lost in the voluptuous heat of his tongue savaging my wind-pipe, my skirt climbing my winged hips, fashionable wool scaling my butt, my succulent surrender mounting the throbbing weight gathering in his dress pants.

"... Mm... mm-mmmmmmmmmmmmmmmmmmmmmmmmmmmmmm...!"

I'm kissing Lucifer. I'm making out with the Angel of Death but I can't stop, my body sexier and more svelte than it's ever been before, my limbs melting into his, my pussy climbing his rock-hard, pulsing spear under his trousers.

"... Mm... mm-mmmmmmm... mm-mmmmmmmmmmmmmmmmmmmmmmmmmmmm..."

My bandeau neckline's around my waist. My legs wrapped are round his waist. The melting place where I go in and in is scrambling for his throbbing spear-head.

He tears his mouth from my frantic lips. Powerful lips, savage teeth, his burning tongue are battening on my tits. The savagery that got him thrown out of heaven, the savagery that sent him plummeting to hell, fastens on my succulent softness and licks and bites and gobbles.

"... Oh... oh..."

Strong teeth fasten on my sumptuous fullness, gnaw at my pounding heartbeat to the voluptuous edge of pain.

"... Oh... oh... oh God...!"

His tongue batters my nipples.

"... Yes... yes..."

He fills his mouth with me and licks sumptuous words straight into my helpless body:

'... If you wish to be a great musician, Constantia, you must go the Other Side...'

"... Yes... yes... ye-eeeeeeeees..."

'... The Shining Path Across the Water...'

"... Please... please..."

'... Find the Key to the Other Side..."

"... Yes... yes... oh God... yes... ye-eeeeeeeeeeeeeeeeeeeeees..."

I know what the 'Other Side' means. I understand what 'the Shining Path Across the Water' involves. He's going to fuck me. He's going to possess my untried body. I don't care. As long as he's quick about it.

His hands cup my butt, hold my feet off the ground, on tip toe, treading water. I get my fingers between our bodies and find buttons and a zip and pull the zip down and his throbbing manhood slips out into my hand—manhood or the Devil's own cock, I no longer care— I'm pumping frantically, my warm palm, that plays soft Chopin chords, pumping hellfire spasms out of his rock-hard cock, my supple fingertips, that coax magic Mozart harmonies from Steinway keys, smearing pulsing pre-cum round and round on his Devil's spear-head.

"... Please... please..."

Strong fingers squeeze and gouge my voluptuous ass-cheeks. A powerful fingertip scours my tight rear cleft, finds my puckered ring's sweet moue.

"... Yes... yes... ye-eeeeeeeees..."

I'll give my soul for his love. I'll sell my soul for one second of his otherworldly love. He can take my helpless ring if he wants. He possesses all of me already.

Sweet words swarm into my mouth. I cry out a song without words, a paean of frantic need.

"... Please... please... fuck me..."

A fingertip slips my thong aside, finds the succulent surrender pulsing between my legs.

"... Please... please fuck me... fuck me hard..."

In an instant I'm rushing towards the brink, going over the edge and plummeting through moonlit blackness and shining fathomless water, his finger inside me, two, three fingers inside me knuckle deep churning my helpless meltdown.

I buck and jerk. My tail-bone kicks.

"... Please... ple-eeeeeeeease...!"

He turns me around and thrusts me face down over the piano. He crushes my face into jangling keys. Thank God. He's going to take me from behind. I spread my legs. I cock the full moons of my shapely ass and show him the sumptuous yearning swamp between my thighs.

"... Please... ple-eeeeeeeeeeeeese... fuck me... fuck me hard...!"

He thrusts his fingers in and out, a three-fingertip phallanx ramming in and out of my pulsing wetness, a cruel trident owning my helpless need.

"... Oh... oh... oh God...!"

I'm wet and engorged and melting voluptuously, *engorged for the Devil*, my virgin wetness a lake of fire overflowing and trickling down my inner thighs.

"... Yes... yes... please..."

His free hand's in my hair, combing forked lightning out of my lustrous mane, my face slipping and sliding on clangorous keys.

"This is how you play the Moonlight Sonata, bitch!"

CLANG CLUNG DANG BANG

Strong fingers grab a silky handful and ram my face into the keyboard again and again. It doesn't hurt. My face is a delirious painting on a wet rag for him to do what he wants with.

CLANG DING RANG RORK

I spread my legs. I cock my butt.

"... Please... please fuck me..."

I'm not on the pill. I've no idea about contraceptives. I don't care. I just need his Devil's seed inside me. I want to die on His throbbing scepter.

"... Please... ple-eeeeeeeeeeeeease..."

His rock-hard cock trawls my supple spine. His throbbing manhood slides up and down my backbone's helpless jerking.

Lucifer's mighty javelin whets its spear-head on my quaking tail-bone. His throbbing tip skims the wet heat where I go in and in.

I shut my eyes.

I am one with my Master.

I wait.

Nothing.

Just a jangle of steel strings dying away.

Only the silence of cruel ivory.

An abrupt metallic sound. Metal teeth knitting with metal teeth. A zip going up.

"... Oh... oh... oh-hhhhhhhhhhhhhhhhhhhhh...!"

I'm climaxing! I'm going over the brink! I'm lost. I'm gone. I'm just a long, voluptuous shudder, bent over my Master's Steinway, his fingers ramming in and out of my pussy.

"... Yes... yes... ye-eeeeeeeeeeeeeeeeeeeeeeeeeeeees...!"

My Master's fingers fly away! They scorn me. My Master's fingers drum on polished teak.

He's sitting back in his armchair! An ankle cocked on one knee! His pants zipped up, his Satanic instrument a mere bulge, massive but hidden, under black, skin-tight cotton.

Maxim's lounging in his easy chair. He peruses my quaking need from across the room. He's a man again, a mere man of the world who's just humiliated a whore, got his money's worth.

My skirt's up around my waist. Some time during... whatever it was that's just happened... an innocent breast slipped free of my bandeau neckline.

I tuck my shapely softness back in. My body goes hot all over. My face is burning. I'm blushing to the roots of my hair. I straighten my skirt, adjust my panties.

He assaulted me. He's just assaulted me! He attacked me. I need to scream. I have to scream. I need to yell for help. I need to pick up my music and get out of this fire-lit torture chamber.

"C Major! Go on!"

"What?"

"You heard me. A C Major scale!"

His tone is cool and imperious. It's as if nothing at all's happened.

"Ey?"

I'm boiling hot. My head's spinning. Maybe nothing did happen.

He snaps his fingers at me.

"C Major! C'm on! C'm on!"

Scales.

C Major.

The simplest scale there is.

I pick up the stool. I sit down. I don't bother to adjust the height of the stool. I begin to play. I'm not sitting straight. My hands are in the wrong position. I squirm and fidget. There's something wrong with my fingers.

"Keep it smooth, can't you?"

I can't concentrate. Not even on C Major. I don't know what I'm doing. Raw yearning's stopping me from sitting up straight, the yearning raw and voluptuous where his fingertips— that master Rachmaninov and flirt with Mozart— found my clit.

"Go on on! Go on! Keep playing!"

Up and down the keyboard, nothing but white keys. C Major. The simplest scale in the book, and I can't even play that properly.

CHAPTER THREE: RECORDING SESSION

When I get home my mother says:

"What happened to your face?"

I check in the mirror.

"... Oh... oh... oh that? That's... nothing..."

There's a nick on my lip, a swollen sting where a black key caught my mouth when he forced my face into the keyboard.

"... It's just a... I... erm... bit my lip, I was concentrating so hard..."

A flicker of consternation crosses my mother's face.

"How was your lesson?"

"... My lesson... oh... oh that...?... my lesson went fine..."

I immediately realize the stupid mistake I've made. If my lesson went fine *Mama will expect me to go back to him for the next one*. She's booked a whole course of lessons. I'd rather die. No way am I ever going to set foot in that fiend's candle-lit torture chamber again. The very thought makes my flesh creep.

Fiend?

I want to laugh out loud.

I nearly laugh hysterically.

What a fool I've been! What a total idiot!

Thinking that puffed-up lecher was Lucifer? Imagining that that hyped-up sex pest was the Devil Himself?!

I must have been out of my mind. I don't know what could have got into me. Satan's rock-hard cock trawling my supple spine? Lucifer's mighty javelin whetting its spear-head on my quaking tail-bone? The Angel of Death's throbbing insistence rimming my succulent need. Splayed, frantic, my helpless surrender pleading for the Devil to fuck me?

It's a joke. A bad joke. It's all just a horrible joke. Herr Maxim Steinhammer the Devil? I want to laugh out loud, except I don't want my mother to see the state I'm in. Herr Maxim is nothing but a beastly predator. A lecher. A heartless abuser taking advantage of a pupil's innocence. Thank God he never actually took me. Thank heavens he never initiated my still-untried body, when I... My face burns. I go hot all over... I can still hear myself pleading with him, I can still feel myself, bent over the keyboard, begging him to... to... oh God! I don't want to think about it!

Well. There's only one thing that's for sure—I'll never sit down at Herr Maxim Steinhammer's Steinway again! Ever! I'll never set foot in that hideous room with that ghastly man ever again!

"Constantia! Darling! What's the matter?"

"... Nothing... nothing's the matter, Mama..."

My mother's eyes fills with worry.

"Perhaps you'd better practice harder, my dear. I hope Herr Maxim doesn't think you're a slacker!"

Mama pushes me so! She's used all her wealth and power to give my career the boost that it needs. It's why my career's been so 'meteoric'.

"Come on, Constanta! Snap, snap! Rachmaninov! Rach Two! Another couple of run-throughs. Right now, before you forget what he's told you! Rachmaninov's Second Concerto! There's your recording session this afternoon!"

My recording session?

This afternoon?

I'd completely forgotten!

With the stress of my lesson it's entirely slipped my mind!

I'm due at the Deutsche Gramaphon Studios at three! To make a recording—Rachmaninov's Second Piano Concerto— for *Deutsch Gramaphon!* The premier classical music label in the world!

"Just one run through, Constantia. So you're ready for this afternoon!"

I stand staring at my Steinway.

The lid's propped up, open, ready.

The keys wait in their obedient rows, Ebony and ivory ready for me to awaken them from their trance. My beautiful Steinway... just looking at it makes me sick to my stomach.

"... No, Mama... I don't need another run through... I'm quite... quite ready for this afternoon... I think I'll just... go and have a shower... I'm feeling... a bit sticky..."

****

The Deutsch Gramaphon studio is in a large, brightly-lit auditorium with state-of-the-art acoustic paneling and sound reflector equipment.

I stand by the podium with Gerard Forsyth, who'll be conducting the orchestra in the concerto, and go through the score with him one last time while the musicians file in.

Chairs clatter. Violinists, flutists, cellists take their seats. Feet shuffle. Music stands scrape. Double bassists perch on their stools. Percussionists arrange their drums and triangles. A piccolo tweets. A trombone jaws.

Gerard says:

"We'll take the opening chords slowly, ey? Agreed?"

The first violinist plays an A and the orchestra tunes up. I suddenly feel even sicker to my stomach than when I went and took a shower and washed the tang of Maxim Steinhammer's fingers out of my pussy.

"Yes. Sure."

Gerard's nice. He's a young up-and-coming conductor, just like I'm a young, up-and-coming pianist. He has nice blonde hair and a refined, sensitive face. His willowy body looks as good in jeans and T-shirt for the recording session as it does in full tuxedo up on the podium at a concert.

"108 bpm. Okay?"

"Okay."

I know Gerard pretty well. We've performed together a number of times, done concertos by Chopin and Mozart and Katchachurian.

"Are you alright, Constantia. You look a bit..."

"... No... no... I'm fine."

I like Gerard. He's destined for a big future in music, the same as me. If I hadn't made a decision to dedicate myself wholly to my career I might even have considered marrying Gerard. He hasn't actually asked for my hand or anything, but I've been feeling him building up to pop the question for a number of months now. If my ravishing touch and singing tone didn't stem from my staying a virgin it's Gerard I might possibly have chosen to lose my v-card with.

The orchestra falls silent. The musicians are all tuned up. The first violinist taps his bow on his music stand and the hush grows deeper.

Gerard looks round at where the sound engineers are sitting behind their banks of monitors and mixers. The chief engineer nods.

A one-hundred-person orchestra, one of the leading orchestra's in the country, each musician on top money, the cost of the engineers and their equipment, Gerard's salary and mine— Deutsch Gramaphon are paying out hundreds of thousands of dollars for the privilege of recording me and Gerard this afternoon. They're placing high hopes on our future success.

Gerard smiles down at me:

"Okay?"

"Yes."

I'm not really concentrating. I'm thinking how nice his blonde cow-lick looks flirting with the generosity of his broad, thoughtful forehead.

I take my seat at the piano, yet another Steinway. The stool's already been adjusted to the perfect height for me.

You don't need to wear anything special to make a recording. I've chosen a nice comfortable pair of white jeans and a white T-shirt. I don't know why I chose white. It just sort of felt right.

Gerard raises his arms to the ready, the baton perched in his elegant fingers. Up on the podium, in his jeans and sweat shirt, he looks really handsome, boyish with his blonde cow-lick but somehow manly too.

It's me who plays the first notes. In fact the first five resounding C Minor chords.

Mama's sitting at the side of the studio. She gives me a thumbs up. She knows it's going to go well, not too many hiccups or reruns. Gerard and I have been rehearsing for several days now with this orchestra of celebrity musicians.

A sudden total silence.

The whole world waits.

Gerard's baton dips.

My fingers sink into the perfectly-chosen, ravishingly-resistant keys.

I play the first chord. C Minor, with an octave in the bass.

The second chord.

With an octave in the bass.

The third.

With an octave in the bass.

The fourth.

With an octave in the bass.

The fifth.

The C Minor swells, fills everything, lifts and rolls outwards on its deep octave foundation.

I suddenly feel a voluptuous sense of relief and freedom. I survived my lesson with Herr Steinhammer. I came through my ordeal basically unscathed. I'm young and talented and beautiful. I'm still a virgin, thank God. I'll put my foot down. I'll refuse to have any more lessons. I'll never see Herr Maxim's ugly face again.

I play.

It's the best I've ever played! I've never pressed sounds like these from obedient keys before.

The black keys bow. The white keys respond to every pulse and stroke of my fingertips.

Magnificent harmonies billow forth into the recording devices, and from them on out into the world beyond. And... I'm on top of the world. I'm a virtuoso! I realize I'm the best ever!

Gerard glances down from his podium, enraptured at my playing, in love with me.

First Movement, Moderato.

Second Movement, Adagio Sostenuto.

I play even better.

Third Movement, Allegro Scherzando.

Better and better.

Every note's perfect. There's no need for retakes or second tries. I'm flying. I soar on angelic wings, I can feel the whole world falling in love with me, not just Gerard's amazed smile.

We reach the second restatement, fortissimo, piano-and-full-orchestra, of Rachmaninov's greatest tune ever. I'm playing the most beautiful theme tune ever written. Grandiose and heartbreaking. Poignant and sublime. The pulsating melody surges upwards beneath my...

... Black electricity knots my fingertips...

... An enraged clangor fills my brain...

... Dark sparks fly from under my touch...

... High voltages shock my fingers into clashes and clatters and hideous staccatos...

... Everything goes black. The brightly-lit room's blotted out in a cloud of billowing darkness...

... I feel sick to my stomach. A terrible emptiness churns in my belly...

... The darkness freezes over. A shivering blackness locks my fingers to jangling notes, freezes my fingertips to hideous claws...

I stop dead in mid flight. The whole orchestra grinds to a screeching halt.

"What's wrong?"

Gerard's eyes look down at me, racked with sudden concern.

"... Nothing... nothing's wrong..."

A current of urgent darkness surges through me. I'm bewitched. I realize at once that he's put me under a spell. Herr Maxim Steinhammer has put me under his spell. Or rather, curse. I've been cursed. By the worst curse ever uttered. I'm damned. I'm in Lucifer's devilish grip. I've been cursed by the Lord of Darkness Himself.

Gerard's got his arm around me. He's massaging my shoulder, patting my hair.

Someone brings me some water.

I'm sobbing like a lost child. I weep my heart out into Gerard's chest. My career's finished. My life's over. I'll never play again.

"Let's call it a day." Gerard's so kind and loving. "We'll try again tomorrow."

Hundreds of thousands more dollars, all for my stupid sake. Mama's fussing. It's over. Everything is over. I'll never play the piano again.

The darkness clears as suddenly as it started.

The black electricity switches off as instantaneously as it switched on.

In the blink of an eye everything is bright and focused and normal again.

I try to smile:

"... No... no... we've got to finish... we must finish this thing today..."

Gerard's reluctant. The engineers are sympathetic. But I get my way. In fact, I'm insistent to the point of hysteria. We must finish the recording right now.

I take a breather and we go back to where the bolt of lightning hit me. We start over again from where the poignant theme comes in.

The darkness is gone. The black electricity has vanished. I'm focused in an absolute clarity. My fingers are once more finding the right notes, the perfect notes, digging the correct resonance out of the grateful keys.

We make it through to the end.

The orchestra claps. They're clapping me!

Even the engineers applaud.

Mama's on her feet; "Bravo! Bravo!"

Gerard hastens to reassure me that my performance was great. He's patting mys shoulder. His conductor's fingers, still gripping his baton, are patting my head through a lustrous tangle of mussed-up hair.

More cries of:

"Bravo!"

"Bravissimo!"

I'm still trembling.

Gerard cuddles me:

"Don't worry, Constantia. It's okay. It was just a blip. In the end you were great."

In the end's not good enough. Okay's no help at all. I've failed. He smiles:

"The engineers will sort it out."

"... Yes, but..."

There's no engineers on earth can sort out what's coursing through my body. There's no sound editing in the world can stop the panic pounding in my heart. Only my teacher can do that. Only my Master can help me now.

I'm going back to see Herr Maxim Steinhammer. I need another lesson.

CHAPTER FOUR: SECOND MOVEMENT

ALLEGRETTO. SKIPPING ALONG WITH THE DEVIL

His rooms are as dark and gloomy as before.

His lips taste of whiskey, battening on mine. My mouth's hot cupid's-bow plasters his mouth's devouring hunger. His whiskey burn plumbs my throat's voluptuous surrender.

My arms are around his neck, my yearning wetness grinding gathering weight into the coiled thing packed inside his pants.

"... Yes... yes..."

Our tongues swoon and grapple. There's a serpent's sting in the corner of my mouth, stretched to take the full savagery of his kiss.

"... Oh... oh... oh God...!"

I'm sobbing on his chest, my butt quaking in his hands under my skirt already, his big hands kneading and crushing my shapely softness, squeezing me against the throb of his awakening power, a power that no mere man could ever muster, that only a Fiend writhing in hell can know.

I cry out:

"What have you done? What have you done to me?"

Only a Force from the Other Side, a Power from the World Beyond could have transfixed me with such black electricity at the recording session. Only an other-worldly Beast could have tripped me up in mid flow and frozen my fingers at my moment of triumph. Only the Brute Force throbbing through his pants into the helpless wetness between my legs could have such power over me.

His laughter comes back cold and cruel:

"What have *I* done to you? I've done nothing, pet. You've done it all to yourself, Constantia."

"What?" I want to scream. "What have I done?"

He shrugs.

"Fame. Fortune. The worm, ambition, festering in your heart. You're as bad as me."

He's a Fiend, and he's preaching to me! He's the Devil, and he's lecturing me!

"No I'm not! That's not true!"

He sneers:

"You're even worse than me!"

I shut the dreadful words out with a fiercer kiss, my plump lips famished, starving for his love, plastering his mouth with luscious poison, my tongue a sumptuous snake yearning in his mouth, drinking up all his succulent secrets, whiskey and cigar smoke and the dreadful things he's thinking about me.

"… Mm… mm-mmm… mm-mmmmmmm…"

I thrust my hand between our thrashing bodies, between my voluptuous writhing and the tolling doom of his powerful body. I find his cock. His trousers are already unzipped, his huge thing lolling raw and irresistible to my scrabbling need.

"… Mm-mmmmmmm… mm-mmmmmmmmmmmmmmm…"

I capture his mouth with my mouth and clasp the stiffening power I need so bad. I wrap frantic fingers round his pulsing dynamo, a monster's or an angel's, I don't care. I pump it with every ounce of love I have inside me.

"… Please… please fuck me…"

Words I thought I'd never utter escape my lips, shocking pleas I never thought I'd cry out in a million years flee from my mouth.

I stroke the pulsing lightning bolt that I want to strike me. My nails comb spasms of darkness from his throbbing spear-head. My manicured, beautifully polished fingernails rake the power aching up and down his whole remorseless length. My virtuoso fingertips draw out a dreadful throbbing from my Master's unforgiving scepter.

I hate the Moonlight Sonata. I'll never play it again. Its lulling moonlight terrifies me. Its lapping darkness overwhelms me. The Other

Side, he called it. The Key to the Other Side. A liquid, shining, bodiless key unlocking horrors.

"... Please... please..."

My fingers are skillful. My fingertips are virtuoso, stroking his throbbing stiffness, twining his merciless tip, my warm palm pumping his rock-hard need to fuck me. He needs me as badly as I need him.

I gaze up into the lightning of his eyes.

"... Please fuck me... I want you to fuck me..."

Imperious hilarity rings around the room.

"Fuck you?" He mocks me. He won't stop laughing at me. "You don't know what you're asking, little girl."

"... I love you... I adore you... I need you..."

His sneer goes up a notch.

"When I fuck a little bitch, *bitch,* she..." He can call me what he likes. I'll be a bitch if he wants me to be. "... *Stays fucked.* Alright? Destroyed. Finito. It's the end. That's it, baby. Forever!"

"... Please, Maxim..."

I don't care if it's the end. I don't mind if it's forever. Finito is better than this fire that's consuming me. I want to be destroyed.

I slither down his body. Nerveless fingers slide down his starched shirt front. Helpless nails claw at unforgiving cotton. Frantic need thrusts me to my knees.

"... I don't care, Maxim... I need you so bad..."

Dread snatches at my heart. *I used his name.* The Devil doesn't like you calling him by His name.

My hand flies away from its frantic pumping. My fingers fly from his raw manhood—no, not manhood, godhood, devilhood—it's too big and raw and powerful, it's too tall and hard and beautiful, my Master's rock-hard need to destroy me is too magnificent for me to even dream of...

".. Please. Please..."

I plead upwards with my eyes.

His face is a cloud of staticking darkness. His eyes glint cruel lightning.

He nods.

My heart stops beating. A swarm of butterflies churns in my stomach. A wave of gratitude breaks over me.

"... Thank you... thank you..."

I put his throbbing spear-head in my mouth.

There's a savor I've never tasted before. A heady richness like potent wheat-germ. The Devil's own seed. A foretaste of the endless desire he's going to slam into me.

His pre-cum's precious. The slick of semen tastes of his succulent largesse. Nectar of paradise or liquor of hell, I can't tell which.

"... Argh... argh... argh..."

I spread the voluptuous slipperiness around his drumming tip with my tongue. I lick gratefully. I gobble frantically. I nip with my teeth. I clamp his godlike rage in a frantic love-bite and wait...

... He doesn't push me away...

... He doesn't even hit me...

... I'm not blasted out of existence...

"... Glurg... gla-aaarg... argh..."

I take his lightning bolt full in my mouth. I gargle his satanic spear down where breathing grows impossible. My succulent wind-pipe melts on his throbbing tip. I gag on helpless need.

"... Argh... argh... glurg... gla-aaaaaaarg..."

His hands are in my hair. The fingers that span Liszt arpeggios and pound Brahms bombshells into shocked keyboards. His hands are big and strong enough to crush the pulsing eggshell of my skull.

"... Argh... argh... argh-lllllllllllllllllllllllllllllllll...!"

I'm cumming.

I suffocate on a tide of ecstasy. The maestro's fingers scoop up big handfuls of lustrous hair and ram my luscious gullet down hard and fast, again and again onto his throbbing shaft.

"... Glurg... gla-aaaaaaaarg... argh... argh-lllllllllllllllllllllllllll...!"

Sometimes his manhood's in my mouth, sometimes it isn't.

He's taking his trousers off. He's stepping out of his briefs. He rips his crisp white shirt off as if it's a hateful rag that's tormenting him.

My heart thumps. The butterflies beat their wings. My heart takes flight. Maxim's going to give me what I want. He's wonderful. He's generous. He loves me. He's going to give me what I need. He's going to give me the only thing I've ever really wanted in my whole life.

"... Yes... yes..."

SLAM

Polished teak slams into polished teak. There's a juddering impact. The whole room shakes.

He's snatched the prop away from under the Steinway's lid! The full weight of grand piano hardwood smashes down shut.

"... Oh..."

His hands are under my armpits, a strong palm crushing a breast, his other hand between my legs grasping struggling wetness, his fingers sinking in, gripping and lifting...

"Ouch!"

He drops me down hard on the Steinway's lid.

Steel strings jangle, felt hammers murmur somewhere under my slithering butt.

He's climbing up onto the piano after me! Butt naked, his powerful chest breathing fast, his ripped pecs glistening in the candlelight, his stallion buttocks flexing, packed desire.

The grand piano murmurs and jangles. It's an altar. His Steinway's a long, black, perfectly polished altar *and I'm his sacrifice.* He's going to fuck me! He's going to fuck me on the piano he thunders out his grand performances on! My heart lifts with delight. I'm my Master's mystical creature he intends to sacrifice on the altar of his satanic lust.

"... Yes... yes... please..."

I'm the greatest virtuoso bitch ever. I'm the most talented up-and-coming slut of all time. Once he's poured his magic into me I'll sit at his side in the pantheon of classical music, the Maestro and his Consort.

".. Yes... yes..."

He lies down flat on his back on the lid of the shut Steinway.

He's panting. His mighty chest heaves and shudders, a prostrate animal in its lust agony.

His huge thighs twitch. Sweat glints in the hairs on his legs.

He's so tall he covers the full length of the piano. Adonis taking His ease. Osiris offering Himself up. His rock-hard thing suddenly huge, too huge, it's way too big, his Scepter a raw unmanageable spear to impale my helpless surrender on.

"... Yes... yes..."

My knees slither on polished hardwood. My palms are too slippery. I have to sink my fingers into a thicket of black chest hair and go up on one knee and arch my split to straddle my destiny.

"NO!"

His roar shakes the room.

"I SAID NO!"

His voice is suddenly terrifying.

"... YOU STUPID BITCH... NO-OOOOOOO... !"

"But..."

He sneers.

"... So pretty... *AND SO FUCKING STUPID...!...* so lovely... AND SO *COMPLETELY FREAKING DUMB!"*

I'm appalled.

"I TOLD YOU, DIDN'T I? FINITO! THE END! *DO YOU WANT TO DIE?"*

"... Yes... no... I..."

He grabs my hair. He pulls me off him, a helpless doll slithering on slippery hardwood, denied the thing she needs most.

His big hands grab my hips. He lifts me and spins me around. He jerks me around a hundred and eighty degrees like a floppy toy in the hands of an angry giant.

I don't know where I am, or what's happening.

"... Oh... oh..."

Hot breath splays my slippery wetness. Whiskey burn slithers between my legs.

I'm sitting on his face!

My knees are on either side of his head, careening on slippery teak, my sumptuous meltdown grinding into his mouth, my hot slick riding his powerful lips, his tongue already inside me licking and jabbing.

"... Oh... oh... oh... oh God...!"

It isn't a tongue.

It's a fang. A long meaty fang coiling and striking at my voluptuous wetness!

"... Yes... yes..."

A tsunami of pleasure breaks over my whole body.

A wolf's teeth find my clit. Sharp. Ferocious. Merciless. Savage teeth pincer my quaking nub, lift me on a surge of helpless sweetness.

"... Please... please..."

I jerk and buck on his broad mouth. My tailbone kicks in luscious ecstasy. My delicious meltdown grinds at the jaws of Hell.

"... Oh... oh... oh God..."

His towering manhood throbs and sways right there! In front of my face! I take it in my mouth. I batten on his rock-hard devil-head. I impale my luscious gullet again and again on his thick, tangy, pounding need to destroy me.

"... Argh... argh... argh-llllllllllllll..."

I gargle his pulsing spear-head in sweet throat honey. I gag the sumptuous beating of my heart onto his relentless insistence, my pussy undulating in his mouth, a melting boat on an ecstatic sea going under fast.

"... Glurg... gla-aaaaaarg... argh-lllllllllllllllllll..."

I clamp him between my teeth way down deep. I don't know where I learned to do these things. I sink a savage love-bite into his aching power, deeper than girl has ever bitten, more lost than any woman has ever been lost, and rake upwards with my teeth, comb delicious spasms of delight out of his rock-hard spear.

"... Argh... argh..."

I jerk and buck.

I drizzle a moment's breathless spittle on his throbbing spear-head, spread it around with my tongue, feel him flinch at the savagery of my desire. I moue his huge tip in my luscious hunger and satisfy it again and again. I impale my gullet's sweet surrender again and again and again.

"... Glu-uuurg... gla-aaaaaaaaarg.... Argh... argh... argh-lllllllllllllllllllllllllllllll...!"

My desire's as savage as his. My longing's even more relentless than his. I cum again and again in his mouth but nothing satisfies me. I suck and bite and gobble, a more voluptuous Beast than he, a hotter Animal than he'll ever be, my need more Monstrous, the wildest Bride the Devil's ever had.

"... Argh... argh..."

A clench. A fierce jolt in his rock-hard stake. I feel his sumptuous explosion gathering. His desire is as helpless as mine. If he wants to cum in my mouth he can. If he needs to feast me on his throbbing life force, satisfy this yearning in my throat, so be it. I lick and gargle and drown him in loving desire. I bring him to the brink...

I'm falling off the piano!

He's thrust me away!

Not a drop!

Not a single drop of his hot love to quench my parching mouth.

I'm on the floor, struggling to pull my panties up, straighten my top.

He doesn't want me. He doesn't need me. He's climbing down off the piano, bored with me, totally uninterested.

He nods at the fallen piano stool.

I pick it up and seat myself at the keyboard. I look up at the clock. There's ten minutes left of my lesson.

He nods at the score on the music rack.

The Moonlight Sonata, Op. 27 in c#. Second Movement, Allegretto.

"C'm on! C'm on! You're hour's nearly up!"

"... But..."

"Second Movement! Get a freaking move on!"

My whole body's shaking. My fingers won't work. I feel like I'm going to cry.

Allegretto?

The second Movement of the Moonlight Sonata is even more insulting than the first, a dainty little allegretto skipping along in triple time. The second movement's almost as easy as the first. It's more childlike if anything, the excruciating dah dah dah dah dah dah dah dah dah dah dah dah replaced by a cute little tune for children to skip to.

Dah dah dah DUP dah dah dah *DU-UUUP!*

He makes me play it over and over till I am really crying.

CHAPTER FIVE: TV INTERVIEW

"How did your lesson go, darling?" Mama's voice is anxious. "Why are your eyes so red?"

"... Oh... nothing, Mama... just some dust in my eyes from the street... my lesson went fine..."

"Are you sure?" says Gerard. His kind eyes are full of concern. Gerard's been visiting us a lot lately. Gerard's face is even more worried than my mother's. "What's that...?"

A red mark on my neck where the Beast bit me as I was playing his insulting little practice piece for the umpteenth time, his teeth leaving a last hot signature on my swan-like throat.

"... Oh that... it's nothing... a bite... an insect bite I scratched a bit too much... there's so many insects in this hot weather..."

Neither my mother nor Gerard look as if they believe me. There's similar bite marks on my breasts, but luckily my bandeau just about covers them.

Gerard says:

"I've brought the score over." He shows me the full piano and orchestra score of Beethoven's 'Emperor' Concerto he's brought with him to the house. "I thought we might have a run through it. Get ready for the big night."

The 'big night' is our upcoming concert, in just seven day's time, at Carnegie Hall. Gerard conducting. Me at the piano, playing Beethoven's greatest concerto. We've both made a good start to our careers in classical music, but our Carnegie Hall debut is sure to be the launching pad to even higher and greater things. The 'Emperor Concerto' is supremely difficult, the crown of the concerto repertoire. Next Saturday's concert will be a major challenge, but if our performance is a success the stars are the limit.

A moment's dread flutters my stomach. If there's a smash up like there was during the recording session our debut will be ruined. Another seize-up like the bolt of black electricity that froze me during the final grand, heart-breaking theme, the whole orchestra grinding to a screeching halt... will be a disaster...

I push the thought out of my mind. I'm brilliant. I'm the hottest virtuoso on the circuit. Gerard's up-and-coming too. The concert's sure to be a success. I say:

"... Later, Gerard... we'll have a run-through later... I feel a little bit low... my lesson's tired me out..."

Gerard's been coming round to our house a lot lately, on the pretext of us preparing for the concerting together, reading through the score in tandem, but I have a feeling he has other reasons beside music for being such a regular guest.

I know Gerard likes me, and not just for the bravura of my keyboard technique. Of course he likes me. I'm pretty. I have a nice body. The advertising agency that promotes my recordings makes considerable play of my being the 'supermodel of the keyboard.'

Who knows? Gerard might even be a little bit in love with me. In fact I have a feeling the famous young conductor's a whole lot in love with me. I wouldn't say no. Perhaps I'll even say yes when he asks. I have three or four refusals under my belt already, maybe it's time to say yes to a marriage proposal.

Gerard's certainly handsome, and very talented too. It might be a good idea if we got together. The agency could promote us as a duo, the hunky guy on the podium and his red-hot pianist girlfriend. It wouldn't hurt our sales. It'll get me away from Herr Maxim Steinhammer. At least it will save me from my demon teacher.

Yes. Marry Gerard. Why not? I do really like him and it'll get me out of a scrape.

There's no point clinging onto my old innocence. I may not actually have fucked yet, but I guess my 'purity's been well and truly blown out of the water. Herr Maxim Steinhammer's seen to that.

Gerard comes from a respectable family, nearly as rich as mine. He'll make a good husband.

There'll be no more lessons. That's the main thing. At least this thing with the Maestro will stop. God knows what Herr Steinhammer's done to turn my head, but it has to stop. He certainly isn't God, not even an evil God. He's not the Devil incarnate. That's all hysteria and fantasy, some sort of crazy hold he's got over me. Maxim's just an over-sexed ladies' man, a randy lecher who's taken advantage of an innocent young girl. Thank God I didn't surrender to him wholly.

My body burns, just thinking about it. I feel myself blush to the roots of my hair... I... I did sort of surrender wholly, but thankfully Maxim didn't take me up on my offer. And one thing's for sure—there won't be any more offers. I'll cancel the rest of my lessons. I'll never see the bastard again.

Gerard goes to put the score away. He'd been looking forward to an afternoon together running through the score. He's trying to hide his disappointment but not succeeding very well. I can tell he was hoping for us to spend an afternoon together on the terrace, sipping cordial and turning over the pages of Beethoven's masterwork, pointing out this delectable sostenuto passage, discussing how we'll handle that difficult tutti.

His smile, even masking disappointment, is so fresh-faced and innocent I say:

"No. I've changed my mind. Saturday's our big night. We need to be ready. Let's have a look at the score one more time. Out on the terrace. It's not so hot as it was earlier." I ring the bell. "Clara! Some of your delicious lemon cordial!"

****

My decision to share a few hours score reading with this lovely man proves to be a good one.

Gerard and I sit together on the terrace drinking lemon cordial, agreeing some important changes to the second movement, Adagio un poco mosso, leaning comfortably close across the little white wrought-iron table, my smooth, shapely forehead at moments almost touching his broad, thoughtful one.

My exhaustion vanishes. My anxiety dissipates. I push the horrific details of my last lesson out of my mind. I cling to the fact that I didn't finally succumb. I'm still a virgin. That's the main thing. I came perilously close to succumbing but something luckily at the last moment saved me. I'm still whole. Still intact. My sensational body is still basically untried. Herr Steinhammer didn't want me and I'm glad he didn't want me. I've kept hold of the untried beauty that Gerard's eyes tell me so plainly he adores.

****

Life grows calmer, and happier, as the big day approaches. Gerard and I rehearse every day. With the Philharmonia itself! Our rendition of Beethoven's Emperor Concerto gets steadily better, run-through by run-through. I can already hear next Saturday's rapturous applause, the glowing reviews showering down on us from the most influential critics in the land.

If a difficult arpeggio causes me a momentary anxiety, if a sudden accelerando brings with it a brief flash of black electricity across my vision, Gerard is always there for me, up on the podium, leading the orchestra towards a triumphal climax, his thoughtful eyes and generous smile there to reassure me.

The concert's bound to be a success. There's so much advance publicity it seems everyone's talking about Saturday night. Posters in every subway station. Gerard and I up in lights on Broadway. Full-page photographs in every newspaper and music magazine, the pictures making great play of my beauty but I don't mind. Many of the images are of Gerard and me together, classical music's hottest couple.

I'm even interviewed live on Music Today, an hour long interview shot live here at home, with clips of me playing popular piano classics—they ask for the Moonlight Sonata but I insist on Mendelssohn's 'Song Without Words'—and answering questions about my career and personal life.

The interview airs on a Friday night, the night before the concert, ten o'clock, only on a cable channel, but it's exactly the publicity my career needs.

Gerard comes over to watch it with me and Mama at our house.

My mother orders drinks and finger food and we sit back to enjoy the interview in our palatial living room, Gerard next to me on the couch, his broad shoulder managing to nestle itself comfortably against mine.

Mama dims the lights and switches the TV up.

The Music Today theme music, and the interview starts running

Me being asked deliciously easy questions by one of the top TV classical music commentators.

Even my mother's amazed.

"Oh! Heavens above! You're *so-ooo* photogenic, my dear."

I guess I am. My high chiseled cheekbones and full lips and retroussé nose look radiant in the subdued cinematic lighting.

Gerard nudges my shoulder.

"Poster girl for classical music!"

I laugh.

"No I'm not!"

But I am really. I chose a full-length white evening gown for the interview. I was worried it might be a bit too formal for a TV chat but it shows off my voluptuous body so perfectly no one could possibly blame me for choosing it. And when I'm playing for the interviewer—I perform four times during the hour—the long silk robe flowing over the stool, white spaghetti straps straining on my toned shoulders as I attack a difficult passage—when I play the effect is stunning.

"We couldn't have asked for better publicity," says my mother. Mama's always taken an active role in my career.

"Wow!" says Gerard, switching up the sound.

I'm playing 'Song Without Words', my head bowed gracefully over the keyboard, a lustrous tangle of silky blonde hair flirting with the thinnest of shoulder straps, note after perfect note caressing my fingertips as I play, one shoulder strap slipping...

... Oh...?

... A shoulder strap slipping round my elbow...?

... My other shoulder strap slipping too...?

... Tugging at my other elbow...?

... The risqué neckline breathing, stirring *slipping down*...!

... White silk releasing my nipples and sliding down over the sumptuous softness of my breasts... my perky nipples...!

Stop!

No!

This isn't happening!

The piano prop snatched away. The lid coming down with a mighty SLAM!

... My naked bottom's bucking... shucking off a ruck of white silk...!

... Slipping out of my evening dress like a snake out of its skin and I'm...

... Stark naked...!

... I've kick the dress off...!

... Sumptuous wetness glistens between my legs. I climb onto the lid of the piano... the music still playing... dah dah dah dah dah dah dah dah dah dah dah dah... not 'Song Without Words'... DAH DAH DAH DAH DAH DAH DAH DAH DAH DAH DAH DAH... and I'm crawling across the piano lid, my succulent pussy lips parting, my toned butt quaking to the rhythm of an invisible tongue... my gash's luscious lips pressed against throbbing emptiness... jerking... bucking... my hot fist pumping an obscene void... my hot swamp quaking on an unseen mouth... my helpless love cries growing louder and louder... '.... please... please... fuck me...!... I want you to fuck me hard...!' even louder than the DAH DAH DAH DAH DAH DAH DAH DAH DAH DAH DAH DAH...

I stare around in terror.

Mama's leaning back in her armchair, smiling at the screen, a look of managerial satisfaction on her face.

Gerard's smiling blissfully at the lurid wetness slithering on polished teak. His beautiful eyes gaze approval at the obscene twining and thrashing on the piano lid.

'... Please... please... I love you... I adore you... I need you... please fuck me... I want you to fuck me...'

I'm hallucinating. It's only a hallucination. It's just a vision, blocking out the real world. He's tormenting me. He won't leave me alone. His power over me is absolute. He'll destroy me before he ever leaves me be!

"Pet?"

My mother's voice turns panicked.

I'm on my feet. I cross the room. I'm rushing out the door. I have to get out of here. Out of here and everywhere.

"Constantia?"

I'm clattering down the stairs. They can't stop me. Nothing can stop the horror that's pursuing me.

Outside it's dark.

The streets are hot and empty.

My trainers patter on warm concrete. My jeans are already soaking, the crotch drenched in sweat or helpless desire, I've no idea.

CHAPTER SIX: THIRD MOVEMENT

PRESTO AGITATO. THE DEMON STORMS

Candle grease gutters in brass sconces. The reek of whiskey and cigars. The grand piano stands ready and waiting.

I'm ready and waiting too.

I sway on five inch heels. Silver sequins whisper luscious secrets to my perky butt, the fuck-me hem of my miniskirt halfway up my voluptuous curves.

My peek-a-boo neckline breathes forth sumptuous promises.

In this all-nite city you can always find a 24/7 retailer to sell you the outfit you need.

He's splayed in an armchair, a glass of bourbon balanced on the arm.

He looks me up and down.

I look good. Purple highlights twine in my artfully tangled mane. The beautician's threaded some extra darkness into the stunning arch of my eyebrows, dusted heightened color into my chiseled blush, traced luscious cherry into my already delectable lips.

In this all-nite city beauticians work long hours.

His dark eyes flash beneath their leonine brows. His predatory smile lounges in the virile thicket of his black beard. His gaze lingers where snickering sequins give way to a glimpse of glistening thong.

"Ah!" His purring rumble's more predatory than ever. "My favorite pupil." I think I'm his *only* pupil, not just his favorite. No one else would be insane enough to come to him at this time of night. "What does my favorite pupil want to practice tonight?"

My mind's made up. He's going to fuck me properly. I've come to a decision. This time he's going to initiate me the way a girl wants to be initiated. At the core of her hot need. At the molten entrance to her heart. No more playing games with my helpless desire. No more blow-jobs, no more soixante neuf and all the other kinky things he's done to my willing body. Practice tonight? Tonight Maxim is going to make a woman of me, the most stunning virtuoso to ever seduce an audience, whether he likes it or not.

"Oh..." I saunter to the piano. His Steinway stands waiting, the keyboard open, an immaculate row of ebony and ivory. "... Third Movement tonight. Presto Agitato."

At last something worthy of me. Finally! Music befitting my tempestuous heart. The Third and final movement of the Moonlight Sonata is a tumultuous torrent of unbridled energy, a torrent of notes, sweeping away all moony dah dah dah dah dah dah dah dah dah dah dah dah and cute little skipping songs.

I run a damson fingernail down shivery ivory. The beautician's done my nails real nice.

"Presto Agitato? Careful, Constantia."

My heart's racing. I murmur:

"I know who you are."

He laughs.

"All the more reason to take care."

I plant both hands, palms downwards on the keyboard, press my full weight into expectant ivory so slowly and gently not a single note dares sound. I whisper:

"Great artists don't take care. Virtuosos take risks."

I sink my weight into the keyboard and bend at the waist. Silver sequins catch their breath, inching up my sumptuous softness.

His voice is stern.

"I told you. You don't know what you're talking about."

"... Please..."

I stare into the heart of the piano, at steel strings and felt hammers, and cock my butt, spread my legs a little, show him the succulent gift straining at my G-string, the yearning moisture even the Devil Himself can't resist.

He's suddenly angry:

"I told you already. When I fuck a little bitch, *bitch*...! She stays fucked. Destroyed. Finito. It's the End. That's it, baby. Forever!"

I spread my legs, cock my butt a little higher, feel sweet moisture tingle.

"... I want it... I want forever..."

His armchair creaks.

I daren't look round.

He's on his feet. Somewhere behind me.

I feel his breath on my shoulder, a whiskey burn bedewing my winged nakedness. He tousles my hair. His hiss scorches my ear:

"... So pretty and so stupid... !... *so lovely and so completely fucking dumb!*"

"... I don't care... I love you... I need you to fuck me... I need you to fuck me hard...!"

His voice is a dangerous mutter in the darkness somewhere behind me.

"I'll teach you to love me, bitch. I'll give you fuck me hard!"

"Oh..."

Something whisks across my bottom. A sharp tickle like dry ferns swaying in an angry wind sizes up my voluptuous shapeliness.

"... Oh...?"

It's a whip. I know it's a whip, some sort of cat-o-nine-tails, before it even lifts and caresses my butt with a sharper, headier sting.

"Ouch!"

"You want it do you?"

"... Yes... yes..."

"The Moonlight Sonata. The Key to the Other Side."

"... Whatever... please... please..."

The leather thongs ride my ass so casually I can almost count them... one... two... three... four... five... six... seven... eight... nine... yes, nine inquisitive thongs with knots at the end leisurely sizing up my perfect butt. A cat-o-nine-tails.

Slash!

"Ow-www...!"

The next tickle stings hotter. Cruel leather burns. Fiery knots ask burning questions of my toned softness.

Slash!

"Ow-eeeeee...!"

I hold my breath and wait. I shut my eyes and press down harder into the keyboard. I can feel how perfect my ass is, how deliriously soft and sumptuously toned in his unforgiving eyes.

Slash!

"OW...!"

One slash follows quick on the heels of the first... the next lingers for what seems like hours, making me wait... it's impossible to tell when the next blow's about to fall.

Slash!

"OUCH!"

It's impossible to tell when the next blow's going to fall but each slash is getting stronger than the one before, stinging deeper with a steady, merciless precision.

SLASH!

"OW-WWW!"

The stinging begins to feel wet. The burning turns slippery. My skirt's up around my waist offering fresh fields of softness, my tail-bone jerking like a tremulous knuckle, bucking to each fresh fiery seizure of pain.

"... OW-EEEEEEE... OW... OW... YES... YE-EEEEEEES..."

I'm his moon girl. He's the Devil and I'm his Moon Woman, my butt two full moons, two blood moons, rising on a horizon of crimson ecstasy.

"... Yes... yes... please..."

SLASH!

"OW-WWWWWWWWWWWWWWWWWWWWW...!"

He's panting.

"Like that do you, bitch?"

"… Yes… yes…"

I don't care who he is. I'm the Devil's bitch if he wants.

There's a terrible pause. He draws the hot thongs slowly, inch by inch, between my legs, up the pulsing wetness of my helpless surrender.

"… Yes… yes… please…"

He lubricates his cat-o-nine-tails in my helpless juice.

Ready, are you?"

"… Please… ple-eeeeeease…"

SLASH!

"OW-EEEEEEEEEEEEEEEEEEEEEEEEEEEE…!"

There's a hawking sound in his throat.

In a crimson blur I feel a gob of warm wetness, Satan's spittle, land on my butt. It trickles down my stinging curves, the coolest ointment ever, the sweetest liniment in the world, soothing the sharpest pain.

Saliva trickles down my taut, toned cleft. It puddles in my ring.

At concerts, when he strikes a single note, one solitary key, in a pause before the finale or a pianissimo moment in a clangorous crescendo, Her Maxim always uses his middle finger, his third finger with the big signet ring on it, his middle fingertip alone in an infinity of silence.

"Ouch!"

He works it into tight, pulsing muscle. He eases it into the my cute ring's frantic vice.

"… Ow… !… oh… oh…!"

His voice is a murderous hiss:

"Want me to fuck you, do you?"

"… Yes… please… ple-eeeeeeeeease…"

His finger's in deep. A hairy knuckle twists in my rear crack.

"… Please… please fuck me…"

The stinging turns to ecstatic fire bathing my butt in healing flame. I quake and throb in his hand.

"… Yes… yes…"

His finger slips out. I hold my breath. His fingertip's replaced by something bigger and thicker and harder and much more terrifying.

"... Oh... oh... oh God...!"

He pushes my face down into the keys. I bathe my eyes, my forehead, my mouth in jangling ivory and sharp ebony, my butt quaking on his big cock savagely skewering my rear passage, easing in inch by merciless inch, taking total possession of my voluptuous butt.

"... Oh... oh... oh yes... yes... ye-eeeeees..."

The keyboard slews. The piano lurches. No. It's only my helpless surrender swiveling on his massive cock, surrendering to the throbbing power sinking into me, making his resistless power my own.

"... Yes... yes..."

I'm so grateful to have his throbbing scepter inside me I don't care that it's not the place where I need Him most. I don't mind if it's Satan Himself who's fucking my butt as long as I make his relentless power my own.

"... Oh... oh... oh God... yes... yes..."

He takes me by the hips. The hands that seduce Chopin and Mendelsshon, that thunder out Brahms and Rachmaninov, grab my hips and hold me where he wants me.

The piano jangles. It murmurs steely dissonances. Hammers rattle. There's a roaring noise in the sound box as Satan grips my winged hips and slams pile-driver after savage pile-driver into my ass's pulsating surrender.

"...   Ouch...   ow...   ow-www...   yes...   ow-wwwwwww... ye-eeeeeeeeeeeees...!"

I rut on his merciless power. Hot undulations grip hold of me, riding on the Devil's merciless prong.

The roaring noise in the piano grows louder and louder, a deafening echo takes hold of the helpless instrument.

"... Yes... yes... oh God... yes... ye-eeeeeeees...!"

I'm cumming. I'm climaxing helplessly, a morsel of ecstasy quaking on his big skewer... he doesn't even notice my spasms of pleasure... he doesn't respond to my ecstasy the slightest... not one twitch or jolt of feeling... just this merciless ride on his rock-hard scepter... second by second... minute by minute... on and on... infinity feels no pleasure... eternity never stops!

"... Yes... yes... oh... oh... oh God...!"

I cum again and again. I'm not even fingering my pussy any more. I don't dare. I buck and jerk on this savage force from the Other Side spearing into me hard and fast and deep, driving me out of my mind, over the brink again and again and again.

"... Yes... yes... Ye-eeeeeeeeeeeeeeeeeeeeeeeeeeees...!"

It's finally over.

I'm slumped over the keyboard panting.

He's pulled out. He's gone but my ass is still on fire. My high heels wobble on slippery parquet. My skirt's up round my waist. My naked breasts are tangled in the music rack. I need to go home. I have to get out of here. I can barely stand.

I collapse onto the stool.

"Ouch!"

Antique leather upholstery stings and burns under my helpless wetness.

He's back in his armchair, sipping whiskey.

"Play!"

He's remorseless.

My fingers slither along the keyboard. My nails scrabble on slippery ivory, sharp ebony.

I'm playing.

The music pours from my fingertips in a wild, ecstatic torrent, *presto agitato*, a surging rush of the most passionate music ever written.

CHAPTER SEVEN: THE MOONLIGHT SONATA, OP. 27 IN C#

CROSSING TO THE OTHER SIDE

I stagger in at around eleven the next morning. I can barely keep my eyes open. My whole body aches. Walking's difficult. My butt's still on fire.

"Constantia! What happened? Where have you been?"

Mama's eyes are wild with worry. The concert's this evening. I'm due on stage in eight hours' time. My mother's invested a lot of time and effort in my career and now it's all being threatened.

I don't know what to say.

"... Nowhere... nothing's happened..."

Gerard's still at the house:

"Are you okay? What's wrong? You look..."

His eyes are wild with concern:

I know how I look. I must look terrible. My hair a mess. My eyes red. My body throbbing from head to toe. It's lucky I didn't throw away the jeans and T-shirt I rushed out of the house in last night. At least I haven't tottered in in the torn sequins and high heels my teacher fucked me in, but I still must look a fright.

"... No... no... I'm fine... just a bit tired... a little sleep and I'll be right as rain.."

I yearn to just collapse into bed and shut my eyes and never open them again.

"What happened? Last night? You dashed out of the house. We couldn't find you anywhere."

"... Oh... oh nothing... it all just... it all just... you know... got a bit on top of me... the concert... the publicity... people's expectations..."

Lying comes easily. I'll do anything just to collapse into bed and go to sleep and shut last night out of my mind forever. The lies slip out effortlessly, but neither my mother nor Gerard look as if they believe me any more.

"There's so much to do..." Mama.s fussing. She's frantic. "... Your hair... your gown..."

"My gown?"

"You still haven't chosen what you're wearing for your big night!"

"... Oh... oh... anything will do..."

Choosing a gown is the last thing on earth I want to think about

"Anything will not do!"

My mother nearly screams.

Gerard's staring at my face.

"Constantia! What is it? What's happened to your face?"

He's staring at me so hard for a second I wonder if I'm sprouting horns. Are a pair of fangs jutting from the corners of my mouth? But it's just the darkness threaded into my eyebrows, some eye shadow that didn't wash off.

"Just leave me alone, will you? It's nothing! Just some... I need a sleep, that's all. Is a couple of hours' sleep too much to ask? Wake me at three. A couple of hours' sleep and I'll be fine!"

****

Miraculously, a couple of hours' sleep and I do feel fine. No dreams, good or bad, trouble my slumber. I wake refreshed.

Gerard's worried that we won't have time for a last rehearsal but I've awoken with enough fresh energy to reassure him that everything will be okay.

My recollections of last night are so bizarre and fanciful it's almost as if they've from another, far-away world. The things Herr Maxim did to me are somehow lightweight, bodiless, the sort of fantasies you can play with in your mind without coming anywhere near real danger. Besides. There's so much to do! There's no time to fret or wonder.

First my hair.

My hair's so strong and lustrous, a quick wash, some waves put in at the back and I'm crowned with my usual sensational mane.

A manicure.

These fingers will be playing the Emperor Concerto tonight.

The manicurist scrapes the remains of last night's damson out of my cuticles. A polish and some transparent hardener and they're once more the two loveliest hands ever.

Finding something to wear takes a little more time.

Mama goes for empire line evening gowns, swags of purple and gold-laced satin.

Gerard fancies something shorter and more simple.

I look nice in both styles but eventually put my foot down and walk from the couturier in a long white flowing gown, tight at the top with a plunging neck-line—my figure has always helped me in my career up till now— the silk tight-fitting to below my hips then loosening into simple but sumptuous waves of ankle-length skirt.

"I'll wear it to go!"

I have to wear it to go. We've left everything so late there's no time to go home. It's seven o'clock already, only an hour till Gerard and I are due on stage.

Mama's flustered. I reassure her:

"It's better this way, Mama. From beauty salon to stage! No time to sit around and worry!"

My mother doesn't look convinced but she can feel my excitement, see how my eyes are shining. She bucks herself up.

When we get to Madison Square Garden the audience is already gathering. Crowds of people are socializing in the piazza outside the auditorium. Expectant eyes glance at Gerard and me as the taxi sweeps us around to the artists' entrance.

The orchestra's already gathered in the crowded space backstage, violinists plucking at fussy strings, double bassists opening their huge instrument cases, brass guys flexing their muscles under tight tuxedos, as if playing the trumpet's a martial art.

Gerard disappears. He's things to discuss with the first violinist.

I'm hurried through to a changing room, small but comfortable, where I can spend the last five minutes looking at myself in the mirror.

Outside, the muffled thunder of five thousand people taking their seats.

A sudden tumult of applause.

I nearly jump out of my skin. I'm not ready yet. By no means am I ready.

It's okay, but. There's an overture first, before the concerto. It's only Gerard warming the audience up with something by Mendelssohn.

Twelve more minutes to go, fifteen at the most.

I shut my eyes and try to concentrate.

... dah dah dah dah dah dah dah dah dah dah dah dah...

... The lapping of water... moonlight shimmering on tranquil water...

... dah dah dah dah dah dah dah dah dah dah dah dah...

... liquid darkness... black depths stirring under lunar radiance...

... dah dah dah dah dah dah dah dah dah dah dah dah...

The dressing room fades away. The thunder of applause turns to the murmuring of a moonlit lake.

"Constantia! Constantia! You're on!"

I hear Mama's voice somewhere, but when I open my eyes she's gone.

The thunderous applause is more distant now, much quieter, because I'm slipping down a corridor, pressing at the bar of a fire door.

The fire door opens.

The night air is warm on my face.

Traffic noise, a dog's distant barking, join the quiet thunder of applause from inside the auditorium but all I can hear is...

... dah dah dah dah dah dah dah dah dah dah dah dah...

The Moonlight Sonata!

It's everywhere!

It's all around me!

It leads me through midnight streets and dark forests. The neon signs are made of moonlight. The cars sliding by in the fierce glow are creatures scurrying through shadowy bushes

... DAH DAH DAH DAH DAH DAH DAH DAH DAH DAH DAH DAH...

The further I go the louder the moonlight gets, drowning out buses and the airplanes glowing miles up in the radiant midnight.

My heels click on concrete and sink into the mulch of forest paths, the trees growing denser as I go, every leaf glossy in the moonlight.

... DAAAH DAAAH DAAAH DAAAH DAAAH DAAAH DAAAH DAAAH DAAAH DAAH DAAH DAAH...

I emerge from shadows onto a moonlit lake, a sheet of radiant purity lapping at a bank of sand and smooth pebbles.

White silk presses to my thighs as I hurry forward, a silky hem caresses my ankles as I push on, molten moonlight shimmering on my shoulders and pulsing white hot in my plunging neckline.

A boat waits at the bank. A small rowboat with pillows and cushions decorating its simple planks.

... DAAAAAAAH DAAAAAAAH DAAAAAAAH...

The music roars in my head, drowns out the roaring of the stars.

Or is that roaring his voice?

"At last!"

His tuxedo blazes in the moonlight. His tailcoat is shimmering darkness beautifully cut. He's dressed in the ensemble he wears for his grandiose concerts.

His dark eyes are lustrous. A royal smile plays with the virile thicket of his beard. He's the most handsome man I've ever seen, or ever will see.

He hands me into the boat. It rocks under my high heels.

The planks and cushions are real.

The tiny rowboat lurches, sways, dips in the water as I get my balance.

He pushes off and leaps in after me. Three hundred pounds of rippling muscle that slammed me into the keyboard, the ferocious weight he sank into my rear tunnel, and the rowboat doesn't even waver as it slides forward, moonlit thistledown could weigh it down deeper than he.

Rowboat?

There's no oars!

The rowlocks are empty. Our boat has no oars, yet it's shooting forwards over the water, its bow parting a wake of rippling moonlight.

"... Oh..."

He takes me in his arms and we kiss.

My succulent cupid's-bow battens on the raw power of his lips, plasters voluptuous hunger on his irresistible lips. My tongue's in his mouth, taking his muscular mouth meat in deep and hard and sweet till breathing gives way to ecstasy.

My arms are around his neck, the boat rocking helplessly as I take his tongue into the back of my throat and lock it there with my sumptuous hunger.

We're kneeling. That's why the boat is rocking so much. We're kneeling on cushions and damp planks, my slim voluptuous virgin body crushed against the stupendous beating of his heart, against the rock-hard force throbbing between his legs.

"... Mm... mm-mmmmmmm... mm-mmmmmmmmmmmmmm..."

He draws his mouth away:

"I warned you. Don't say I didn't warn, Constantia. Destroyed. Finito. The end."

"... Yes... yes..."

"When I fuck, she stays fucked!"

It isn't hubris. It's no idle boast. The raw power pulsing between his legs, he means every word he says.

"... Please..."

It's me that's rocking the boat, not him. The waves of longing surging through my body are too powerful for me to keep still.

The shoreline's gone. The bank's fallen away behind. The boat's lurching from side to side on a sheet of molten moonlight.

"... Please... please fuck me..."

Strong hands cup my butt, drawing me tighter against his aching need of me... yes... need... he needs me... this Devil... no... this God... Osiris... Adonis... needs me with every ounce of his love's infinitude...

My ass jellies in his hands, quakes in the warm palms that shaped the world. My helpless curvaceousness quivers beneath the fingers that set the stars in their places and appointed the sun its role in the sky.

There's no sun now, just endless darkness rocking our little boat to the ... DAAAAAAAH DAAAAAAAH DAAAAAAAH... roar of the moonlight.

He pulls my dress up around my waist. Virtuoso silk gathers around my hips.

His smile is beautiful in the moonlight, his fingers finding my sumptuous wetness. He registers the fact that the country's hottest young virtuoso isn't wearing any panties, that she knew this was going to happen all along.

His fingers slip into voluptuous moisture. His fingertips stir the helpless moonlight pulsing in his moon girl's frantic need.

"... Oh... oh... oh God...!"

I unzip his pants. Such mundane actions still to be done here on the radiant entrance to the Other World! I get his zip undone and take out my pulsing, rock-hard prize.

He lays me down on my back, gently, thoughtfully. The cushions are comfortable.

I'm hot and wet, but surely he's too big! I sling one knee up on the right hand gunwhale. The boat rocks violently. For an instant my high heel's flapping in freezing water. I get my other knee over the left hand gunwhale. I spread myself wet and yearning for my ultimate bliss.

"... Yes... yes..."

The monstrous spear-head that savaged my ass, bent over his keyboard, locates my molten entrance with a swift, sure, gentle lovingness. The yearning tip of his infinite force spreads folds of sopping heat, parts the shining lake between my legs with infinite tenderness.

"... Oh... oh... oh God...!"

I wrap my legs around him, lock his stallion tail-bone between two Jimmy Choo high heel strappy sandals, and lift myself onto his pumping prong. Down and down and down. I can't tell if he's sinking into me or if I'm sinking into him, just that the boat's jerking and bucking beneath us with the force of our love-making and that he's giving me everything I've ever wanted.

"... Oh... oh..."

My butt kicks on soft cushions. My tailbone bangs on creaking planks. For long periods he's nailing me into the bottom of the boat so hard I'm sure our tiny craft will split and the waters devour us. For even longer periods I'm rutting on his royal scepter, cumming again and again, melting again and again on the sweet pile-drivers he's slamming into my sopping depths.

"... Yes... yes... oh God... yes... ye-eeeeeeeeeeeeeeeeeeeeeeeeeeeeees...!"

The sky is lightening. There's a new brightness adding its breathless presence to the radiance of the moon.

"... Please... please... fuck me... fuck me hard...!"

It's dawn. Morning is breaking. My split is a mess of helpless wetness. Hot juice is healing our last lesson's welts on my butt... and he still hasn't cum...

... This will go on forever...

... Our love-making won't stop for all eternity...

I'm screaming:

"... I love you... I love you so much... please... ple-eeeeeeeeeeeeeeeeeease.."

"FU-UUUCK!"

The jolt that goes through me tips the boat up on one side.

His cock slams into me, throbbing and twitching, his exploding spear-head fixing me in time and space.

"... Yes... ye-eeeeeeeeeeeeeeeeeeeeeeeeeeeees..!"

Water's pouring in over the side.

The pillows are already sodden. A cushion floats away.

The lake pours in.

Our boat goes over. We're drowning. Locked together, our bodies plummet. I'm a moon girl wrapped in the arms of endless darkness dropping through bottomless water, his indomitable spear pumping throb after throb of life force into me.

****

It's full daylight when I come round.

The lake shimmers in sunlight.

The treetops on the far bank are green and leaf-perfect.

I'm lying on warm grass on the lake's bank in my silk concert gown.

My hair's dry. So is the warm silk stirring on my thighs. It must have been a dream. There's an aching warmth between my legs but it can only have been a dream.

I stand up. I sway a little on my high heels, but I'm okay.

I brush a twig off my hip.

Somewhere beyond the trees, above the chirruping of birds, I hear the squeal of a bus's brakes, the rumble of traffic. I'm in Central Park, New York.

****

"Constantia!" Mama's full of her usual lecturing anxiety. "You'll have to stop running off like this! It's not polite!"

"We were worried about you," says Gerard.

His eyes are doing their best to look worried but the worry's being overwhelmed by his big, broad joyous smile.

"Just dashing off again!" scolds my mother. "After such a triumph!"

"Triumph?"

"Don't act stupid, girl. I'm going to have to find you a psychiatrist if you won't start facing up to things!"

"What things?"

"Our concert," says Gerard. "The Emperor Concerto!"

"... But... but that's impossible..."

"Oh ho! Therapy for you, my girl. If you can't face reality!"

"Especially such *nice* reality!" says Gerard.

I'm so flabbergasted he picks up the morning newspapers and flicks through to the various Arts Pages to show me:

EPIC EMPEROR!

MLLE DE VAUGHAN GIVES STELLAR PERFORMANCE!

CONSTANTIA DE VAUGHAN SENSATIONAL IN BEETHOVEN'S EMPEROR CONCERTO!

I'm struck dumb.

"... But... but... what's that...?"

A headline mocked me, flicking past too fast.

I turn back to the front page:

"What...?"

MAESTRO DROWNED

"Ey?"

VIRTUOSO FOUND DEAD

I make myself read:

... Early this morning the body of Herr Maxim Steinhammer, the renowned concert pianist, was discovered washed up on the shore of the lake in Central Park...

Don't miss out!

Visit the website below and you can sign up to receive emails whenever Saskia Lane publishes a new book. There's no charge and no obligation.

https://books2read.com/r/B-A-MOWZ-ZXBQC

BOOKS 2 READ

Connecting independent readers to independent writers.

Did you love *Moonlight Sonata Op. 27 in C# BDSM*? Then you should read *Riding a Monster Wave at BDSM Beach*[1] by Saskia Lane!

[2]

Gracie's an up and coming surf champion. Young, beautiful and attractive, she's ridden the Banzai Pipeline and the monster waves of Teahupoo. Tipped to be the next US Open champion Gracie has the world at her feet. So when legendary surfer Clancy O'Rourke offers to give her lessons, Gracie's got it made. Clancy however has some strange ideas— that he's Poseidon, the God of the Sea, and that Poseidon needs a new Goddess to be His mate. Is Clancy just an over-sexed dreamer, or do his stunning physique and prowess on a surfboard stem from occult forces? The more explicit his demands on Gracie become, the more her surfing improves till she's ready to ride the hundred foot waves at Praia de Norte, and ride the elemental lust of her supernatural lover too.

---

1. https://books2read.com/u/bzBJOL

2. https://books2read.com/u/bzBJOL

Also by Saskia Lane

cruising for alphas
Taxi Driver Hot Wife
Taxi Driver Hot Wife 2

steamy paranormal romance
Riding a Monster Wave at BDSM Beach
Moonlight Sonata Op. 27 in C# BDSM

Steamy Trials of a Victorian Lady
In His Lordship's Dovecote
In His Lordship's House of Ill Fame
In Their Lordships' Dungeon

Standalone
Where's My Bikini Bottom? And Other Stories
Where's My Bikini Bottom? And Other Stories
Thanks For The Hotpants, Lieutenant
Explicit Creatures on a Hot Night

The Explicit End of the Beach
Losing my V-card with the Wrong Alpha
Getting a Job in My Mom's Boyfriend's Sex Club
Ouch! That Sand's Hot and This Alpha Stud's Too Big